Beauty
and the
Beast

retold and illustrated by

JAN BRETT

G. P. Putnam's Sons
An Imprint of Penguin Group (USA) Inc.

ACKNOWLEDGMENTS

When she was preparing this retelling of *Beauty and the Beast*,
the author read a number of other versions of the story
and found the one by Sir Arthur Quiller-Couch,
published originally in 1910 by Hodder and Stoughton, London,
to be especially helpful.

G. P. PUTNAM'S SONS • A division of Penguin Young Readers Group.
Published by The Penguin Group.
Penguin Group (USA) Inc., 375 Hudson Street, New York, NY 10014, U.S.A.
Penguin Group (Canada), 90 Eglinton Avenue East, Suite 700, Toronto,
Ontario M4P 2Y3, Canada (a division of Pearson Penguin Canada Inc.).
Penguin Books Ltd, 80 Strand, London WC2R 0RL, England.
Penguin Ireland, 25 St. Stephen's Green, Dublin 2, Ireland (a division of Penguin Books Ltd.).
Penguin Group (Australia), 250 Camberwell Road, Camberwell, Victoria 3124,
Australia (a division of Pearson Australia Group Pty Ltd).
Penguin Books India Pvt Ltd, 11 Community Centre,
Panchsheel Park, New Delhi - 110 017, India.
Penguin Group (NZ), 67 Apollo Drive, Rosedale, Auckland 0632,
New Zealand (a division of Pearson New Zealand Ltd).
Penguin Books (South Africa) (Pty) Ltd, 24 Sturdee Avenue,
Rosebank, Johannesburg 2196, South Africa.
Penguin Books Ltd, Registered Offices: 80 Strand, London WC2R 0RL, England.

Design by Annie Ericsson. Text set in Sabon.
The art was done in watercolors and gouache.
Illustration backgrounds airbrushed by Joseph Hearne.
Library of Congress Cataloging-in-Publication Data
Brett, Jan, 1949–
Beauty and the beast / retold and illustrated by Jan Brett. p. cm.
Summary: Through her great capacity to love, a kind and beautiful maid releases
a handsome prince from the spell which has made him an ugly beast.
[1. Fairy tales. 2. Folklore—France.] I. Title.
PZ8.B675Be 2012 398.2—dc23 [E] 2011013311

ISBN 978-0-399-25731-5
1 3 5 7 9 10 8 6 4 2

To Sarinda

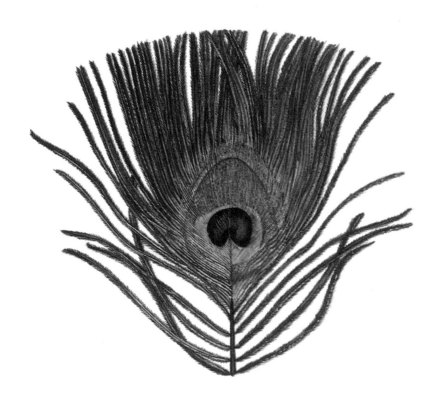

nce upon a time, there lived a merchant's daughter so lovely and
kind that all who knew her called her Beauty.

Beauty lived with her father and two sisters in wealth and with-
out worry. Then suddenly their father lost everything when his ships,
laden with riches, vanished at sea.

The family, now penniless, fled to a country cottage. There they
had to do all the work themselves. Beauty's sisters cried and grum-
bled, but Beauty worked on bravely and tried to comfort her father.

One day, news came that one of the lost ships had survived.
Before leaving for the port, the merchant asked his daughters what
they missed most so that he could bring each of them a present.

The first sister asked for beautiful gowns. The second sister asked for a coach and four horses. Beauty asked only for a rose, since the cottage garden was filled with cabbages.

Upon reaching the ship, the merchant found the cargo spoiled and worthless. Poorer than ever, he headed home through a deep forest until snow covered the path and he was lost. Just when he was too tired to go on, he saw an avenue of orange trees, untouched by the snow, and beyond them a grand palace. He rode toward it, hoping for shelter.

Ornate doors opened wide and the merchant entered a great hall. Strangely, he saw no one, neither master nor servant. But a sumptuous hot meal waited on the table. He ate and fell sound asleep in his chair.

In the morning he woke up and found fresh new clothes and a breakfast of delicious fruits and steaming tea waiting for him. He ate quickly and went outside, where a magnificent horse, all fitted out, stood waiting to take him home.

Just as the merchant was about to mount the horse, he spied a bed of roses. Remembering his promise to Beauty, he knelt and picked one.

Immediately he heard a dreadful angry roar. He looked up and saw a fearsome beast standing above him. "How dare you harm my roses?" the Beast cried. "A rose that is cut can only die. You shall pay for your ingratitude with your life!"

"I have taken this rose only as a gift for one of my daughters, the faithful Beauty," the terrified merchant pleaded.

The Beast glared at him. "I will spare your life, but only if one of your daughters willingly returns in your stead," he growled.

"I cannot send you a daughter," the merchant told the Beast. "But I promise I will return after I bid them good-bye."

The merchant arrived home and gave Beauty the rose. But it was a somber homecoming as he told the grim story of the Beast and his cruel punishment.

Beauty would not hear of her father's return to the palace and certain death. He would never have plucked the rose if it were not for her. She would go to the palace and nothing her father said could dissuade her.

When Beauty and her father reached the palace, the ornate doors opened once again. Fear took hold of them as they went inside.

Suddenly, a fearsome creature, part man, part animal, moved out of the shadows. Overcoming her terror, Beauty stepped forward and greeted him. "Good evening, my lord."

The Beast ignored her and presented her father with a casket containing a fortune in coins and jewels. "You have kept your promise," he growled. "This will restore your house handsomely. Now be gone." And he walked off into the darkness.

The merchant bade a tearful farewell to his faithful daughter. Then the great doors opened and he departed, leaving Beauty quite alone.

BE GUIDED

Thus Beauty began her new life in the palace. A troop of monkeys in court dress appeared to serve her. A charming little dog became her page. A beautiful bird led Beauty to a magnificent bedchamber filled with all of her favorite things. The Beast was nowhere to be seen, and it became clear that she was not in danger.

GRATITUDE

Beauty was free to amuse herself in any way she wished. She spent the day wandering all over the palace and exploring the beautiful gardens, many of them filled with exquisite roses.

That evening, she was taken to a candlelight dinner. As animal musicians began to play, the Beast appeared. Beauty drew back, frightened, but the Beast's courtly manners disarmed her fears.

The Beast reassured Beauty with charming conversation until it grew late. Then he fell silent. At last, he spoke. "Beauty, will you marry me?" Beauty, lowering her eyes, replied, "Pray, don't ask me that."

YOUR HAPPINESS IS NOT FAR AWAY

The days passed happily for Beauty. She even began to look forward
to the evenings and her conversations with the Beast. His thoughtful
ways began to win her trust.

But Beauty dreaded the moment when he took his leave, for he would always ask, "Beauty, will you marry me?"

It grew more and more painful for her to say, "Pray, don't ask me."

Then came a day that passed so happily that when the Beast joined her for dinner, Beauty spoke of her great joy. "The flowers in the gardens have never been more beautiful," she told him. "And the musicians have never played more sweetly."

The Beast again asked for her hand, and with such tender hope she said, "I cannot marry you, Beast. But I will indeed stay here willingly as long as I shall live, if only you will grant me one request. Let me say good-bye to my father and the world I leave behind."

A mournful look came over the Beast. "Return before the moon is full, faithful Beauty, or you will break your poor Beast's heart."

Then he placed a golden ring on her finger and said, "When you wish to come back, turn this ring three times around and say aloud, 'I want to be in the palace of the Beast again.'"

Immediately, Beauty was back in the grand house of her childhood. She watched her father bartering for goods, and her sisters ordering their maids about, just as they had always done.

Seeing Beauty, they all flew to her in amazement. Her father embraced her, and her sisters asked question after question about her strange life in the palace and about the monster who ruled there.

Beauty tried to explain her admiration for the Beast and the wonders of the palace, but even her father did not understand.

The weeks at home went by in a whirl. Laughing young men coaxed Beauty to go out for walks and rides. Her father escorted her to concerts and the opera. Her sisters took her to fancy balls. Beauty had no time to think of the Beast and she completely forgot her promise to him.

One night, after much gaiety and dancing, Beauty fell asleep and
dreamed that she was back in the palace garden, now strangely dark
and cold. She searched and searched, looking for something she had
lost. Then she saw the Beast on the ground, still as death.

Beauty woke up stricken with grief. None of the past weeks meant
as much to her as her life with the Beast. She turned the golden ring
three times around her finger and said aloud, "I want to be in the
palace of the Beast again."

At once, Beauty found herself at the palace gates. She ran into the
garden and there she found the still form of her beloved Beast.

Fearing that he might have left this world, Beauty knelt down and took the Beast in her arms and wept. Her tears, raining down upon his furry head, woke him up, and he looked at her.

"Dearest Beast," she implored, "you must be strong and live so that we may be husband and wife, for I love you so."

When these words were spoken, stars fell from the sky and the palace was illuminated as if by a thousand candles.

Before her, Beauty saw the radiant face of a handsome prince. Her promise to marry the Beast out of love had unlocked a fantastic spell.

Taking Beauty's hand in his, the young prince explained that some years before, a meddlesome fairy, displeased with people for judging others by their appearance, had cast a spell over the palace and everyone in it.

The servants were changed into animals and the prince was turned into the ugliest and most fearsome Beast in the forest. The spell would only be broken when a young maiden fell in love with the Beast and promised to marry him. And that is what Beauty had done.

There was much rejoicing within the palace that night, but no one was happier than Beauty and the prince. They were married the very next day and lived happily ever after.